Rakes

fray

smells good

by Pat Edwards
Illustrated by Joanne Sisson

 sundance

Rabbit's House

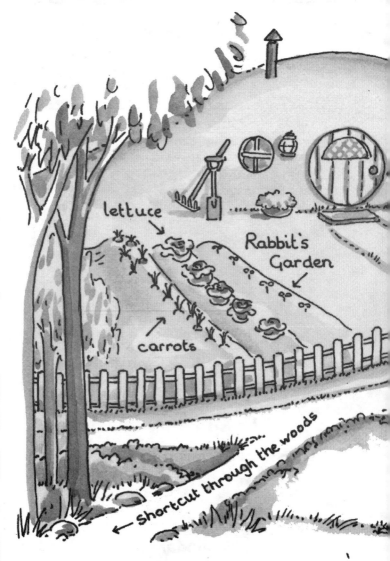

lettuce

Rabbit's Garden

carrots

← Shortcut through the woods

on Windy Hill

to stores

way to creek and Sleepy Corner

Rabbit's Favorite Foods

1. Fresh carrot sandwiches

2. Carrot cake

3. Hot buttered toast

4. Fresh lettuce

5. Peanut butter on anything

I like food that makes crumbs.

Contents

Chapter 1
Bandicoot Smells Toast

Rabbit lived in a neat little house on Windy Hill. Rabbit's friends lived across the creek at Sleepy Corner. It was close enough for them to visit Rabbit whenever they felt like it.

Sometimes Rabbit thought it was too close.

One morning Rabbit felt hungry.
"I know what I want," she said
to herself. "I want some hot
buttered toast."

She got out six pieces of bread.
Then she made six pieces of toast
and buttered them while they
were hot.

"I do like toast all oozy and
   drippy with butter," said Rabbit.
She had just sat down
to eat when someone knocked
at the door.

"Are you there, Rabbit?" called a voice.

Rabbit sighed. "Yes," she said.

"May I come in?" the voice called again.

"Yes, Bandicoot," Rabbit said, putting down her piece of toast.

"How did you know I was at the door?" asked Bandicoot as he bounded into the room.

"I just knew," said Rabbit. "You always come when I'm having something to eat."

Bandicoot sniffed. "Smells like hot buttered toast," he said. "May I have a piece?"

"Oh, all right," said Rabbit. "Help yourself." As she pushed the plate across to Bandicoot, she thought, "That leaves only five for me."

"I do like hot toast, all oozy
and drippy with butter," said
Bandicoot, opening his mouth
wide.

"So do I," said Rabbit.

Rabbit was just reaching for her piece of toast when there was another knock at the door.

"Are you there, Rabbit?" called a voice.

Rabbit sighed. "Come in, Possum," she called back.

Possum peered around the door. "How did you know I was at the door?" she asked.

"I just knew," said Rabbit. "You always come when I'm having something to eat."

Possum sniffed. "Is it hot buttered toast?" she asked.

"Yes," said Bandicoot, who was licking his whiskers. "Have a piece."

"That leaves only four for me," thought Rabbit as she handed the plate to Possum.

"Thank you, Rabbit," said Possum as she took a piece. "I do like hot buttered toast, all oozy and drippy with butter."

"So do I," said Rabbit.

"This is good toast," said Bandicoot. "I'm on my second piece already."

Rabbit looked at the plate. "Only three left for me now," she thought. But just as she opened her mouth for a bite, there was another knock at the door.

"Go away," called Rabbit angrily, "I'm not home!"

Chapter 2
Is Anyone Home?

For a moment, nobody said anything.

Then a little voice called out. "Is that you, Rabbit?"

Rabbit gave a big sigh. "Yes," she called back. "Come in Koala."

"I thought somebody said there
    was no one at home," said Koala,
    opening the door.

"She did," Bandicoot whispered to
    Possum. "I wonder why?"

"No, I'm here," sighed Rabbit.
"And so are Bandicoot and
    Possum. They're eating my toast."

"So that's what I can smell," said
  Koala. She walked over to the table.

"May I have a piece?"

"Why not," said Rabbit, grumpily.
"Help yourself."

"How did you know I was at the door?" asked Koala through a mouthful of toast.

"I just did," said Rabbit. "You always come when I'm having something to eat."

Koala took another bite. "I do like hot toast, all oozy and drippy with butter," she mumbled.

"Everyone does," said Rabbit angrily. "If they're allowed to eat it, that is."

"May I have a second piece too?" asked Possum.

"No," said Rabbit. "What's left is mine."

"But Bandicoot had two pieces," said Possum, "so it's not fair."

"No, it isn't," said Rabbit, "but I don't care."

She picked up one of the pieces of toast and opened her mouth.

"Oh no," cried Rabbit. "Not again!"

The door swung open. "It's Magpie," he said, poking his head through the gap. "May I come in?"

"Why not?" said Rabbit. "Everyone else did. I suppose you want some toast."

Magpie flew over and looked at the plate. "No thanks," he said. "It's all cold and soggy. You should only eat toast when it's hot and all oozy and drippy with butter."

But Rabbit didn't answer. Rabbit wasn't even there. She had marched off, slamming the door behind her.

"I wonder why she rushed out like that?" said Possum, as she and Koala helped themselves to the last two pieces of toast.

"Perhaps she's gone to get some more bread," said Magpie.

"I hope so," said Bandicoot. "I'm still hungry."

Chapter 3
All of Them for Me!

But Rabbit wasn't going to the store. She was on her way to visit Wombat. "I'll tell him I've come to lunch," she thought, "and I'll tell him exactly what I want."

"Six pieces of hot toast, all oozy
and drippy with butter . . . and
all of them for me!"

More Rabbit Stories
by Pat Edwards

Rabbit's Robber

When Rabbit loses all her
furniture, she is sure she has had
a visit from a robber.

But did she?

It Smells Like Friday

Everyone knows that Rabbit
makes carrot cake on Friday,
so what better day for a visit?

But somehow, it all goes wrong!

A Quiet TV Lunch

When Rabbit decides to have
a quiet TV lunch, she doesn't
expect to have to share it with
all her friends.

But that's what happens.